First published in the UK in 2011 by Scholastic Children's Books
An imprint of Scholastic Ltd
Euston House, 24 Eversholt Street
London, NW1 1DB, UK
Registered office: Westfield Road, Southam, Warwickshire, CV47 0RA
SCHOLASTIC and associated logos are trademarks and/or registered
trademarks of Scholastic Inc.
Series created by Working Partners Ltd

Text copyright © Working Partners, 2011

ISBN 978 1407 11712 6

Printed in the UK by CPI Bookmarque, Croydon, Surrey.
Papers used by Scholastic Children's Books are made
from wood grown in sustainable forests.

1 3 5 7 9 10 8 6 4 2

www.scholastic.co.uk/zone

CREEPY CREATURES

RAT PANIC

ED GRAVES

SCHOLASTIC

Collect all the
CREEPY CREATURES

CREEPY CREATURES

RAT PANIC

With special thanks to Tracey Turner

For Toby, the Vultures and the
African Hawk Eagle

This Book Belongs To

The Gnome of Gnome Gardens

Beware!
Never open my Book, unless you
want the Curse of Gnome upon you.
Or is it too late?
Then my creatures will terrify
and torment you.
You can't imagine how scared you will be.
Gnome Gardens belongs to me.
Only me. You shall see. . .

CHAPTER ONE

King Rat

Jamie opened his eyes. Weak dawn light shone into his bedroom through a crack in the thin curtains. Across the room in the other bed, Jamie's little brother, Harry, lay completely buried underneath his duvet.

Jamie yawned. His eyelids drooped, half closed. *Woosh!* A dark-winged shape appeared at the window, silhouetted against the early morning sky. Jamie scrambled up, his heart thumping, wide awake now. He pulled his duvet up to his chin, remembering the horrible bats they'd met two weeks before. But the shape outside the window gave a low hoot as it swooped out of view. *Just an owl*, thought Jamie, feeling his body relax.

The bats had been sent by an evil Gnome who thought their house, Gnome Gardens, belonged to him. Jamie and Harry had found an old book called *The Book of Gnome*, written by their granddad many years ago. When they'd opened it, they had released a curse that meant the Gnome would send his creepy creatures to drive them from Gnome Gardens for ever. The last creatures they had faced were a cloud of evil bats that snatched their friend Milly right out of her bedroom. *We managed to get the better of the bats*, Jamie thought as he settled back down, *but I know we'll see the Gnome again.* They would all have to be brave if they were going to finally defeat their enemy.

Jamie's stomach rumbled loudly. Breakfast. He turned over to see whether Harry was awake yet so they could go downstairs. There was a strange glow around the edges of his brother's duvet. What was it?

"Harry?"

Harry's head, which had a torch strapped to the side of it with a belt, popped out from underneath the quilt. His tousled dark brown hair stuck up in tufts. He was lying on his side, grasping a book.

"What are you *doing*?" Jamie asked.

"What's it look like? Reading," Harry said.

Jamie sighed. "What's the book?"

Harry raised it for Jamie to see the title: *King Rat*. Jamie shivered. Why would anyone want to read about *rats*? He'd never told anyone – not even Harry – but rats were the one animal he couldn't bear. Just thinking about them made his flesh creep.

Jamie's stomach rumbled loudly again.

"Hey, the midnight feast," said Harry, sitting up. "We never got round to eating it."

Of course – they'd brought up some cheese and crackers last night but fallen asleep before they'd had a chance to tuck in.

Jamie reached for the plate, on the floor between the two beds. He stared at it. The crackers were broken and some had disappeared. There were marks on the cheese.

He peered more closely: it looked as though something had been nibbling it. Something with big rodent teeth. Worst of all, Jamie could see tiny hairs stuck to the cheese, and more on the plate. He felt the blood drain from his face.

"Something's been eating our midnight feast!" Harry cried. "Do you think it's mice?"

Jamie didn't reply, but looked from Harry to the book he was holding.

"*King Rat*?" Harry spluttered. "A rat up here? That's disgusting – even worse than mice. You're right, though, those teeth marks look *big*. We'll have to tell Mum and Dad."

Jamie's mouth was dry as he stared at the plate.

"Oh," said Harry, clamping his hand to his mouth. "We can't tell Mum and Dad – rats are the Gnome's next creature."

The pages of *The Book of Gnome* showed the creatures the Gnome would send after them. Once they had defeated the horrible little man's bats, they'd turned the page to reveal an ugly, evil-looking rat.

Jamie forced himself to stop staring at the plate. He swung his legs out of bed. "Come on," he said to Harry. "Mum and Dad won't be up for ages. Let's have another look at *The Book of Gnome* and see what we can find out."

Jamie and Harry crept out of their room and down the stairs. They knew this huge old house well enough by now to avoid the creaky steps, placing their feet carefully on the sides nearest the banister. They were used to the wooden animal carvings that covered the house, too – woodlice, ants and beetles scuttling up the skirting boards, crows swooping from the window frames. Jamie shuddered at one of the carvings: an evil-eyed rat crouched at the bottom of the banisters, ready to spring.

The Gnome's bearded face scowled at them from a wooden panel in the hall. The carving held a secret: when Jamie put his hand over the face and pushed the bulbous, warty nose, a secret door slid open to reveal a passageway. Jamie shuddered, remembering the real Gnome's yellow teeth and nails, his greasy, wispy hair, his filthy clothes and foul stench.

"There are even more cobwebs here than last time," Harry said, brushing one aside. A huge brown spider, as big as Harry's palm, dropped on to his shoulder. He held out his hand to it, coaxed it into his cupped fingers and gently placed it on the floor.

"Not scared of spiders any more?" Jamie asked.

"Not since the Gnome's spider. These little ones can't frighten me after that," said Harry.

Jamie remembered the giant spider they'd met, bigger than both of them and their friend Milly put together. They'd been trapped in its web. Its huge fangs had dripped poison as it crawled towards them.

"We can survive anything now," Jamie said, reaching for the door to the study. But he felt a cold shiver creep down his spine. In his mind's eye he could see an enormous rat, its whiskers quivering, wet nose twitching, long yellow teeth bared. How was he going to cope with *that*?

CHAPTER TWO

The Rat Run

The study door creaked open on rusty hinges, revealing a book-lined room with a great wooden desk in the middle. Coloured light filtered into the murk through skylights high above Jamie and Harry. Red, green and yellow – the Gnome's colours.

Glittering red eyes stared at them. They

belonged to the five creatures carved into a wooden panel on the wall. Three of the carvings faced out into the room: a snake, a spider and a bat, the three creatures they'd defeated so far.

Jamie felt down one of the desk legs for the hidden button that released a secret drawer. His hand traced the length of a carved snake to its head: the button was one of its eyes. "That's it."

A drawer slid open on top of the desk and Harry took out the old, musty-smelling *Book of Gnome*.

Dust motes swam in the red, green and yellow light as Harry opened the book.

". . . The spider . . . the bat," Harry muttered, turning the pages. "Here it is. The rat." He tilted the book to show Jamie.

The picture showed a rat wearing a golden crown on its head between pink, greasy-looking ears. *King Rat*, Jamie thought, *like Harry's book*. The rat had matted brown fur, beady red eyes, and sharp claws on its hairless feet. Its jaws were open, showing long yellow front teeth. A whip-like tail curled around its body. Jamie felt his stomach lurch as he looked at it.

Underneath the picture were printed some words.

"*The worst enemy can make a hidden friend*," Jamie read aloud.

"What does that mean?" Harry asked.

"I don't know. It doesn't help us at all," Jamie said. "I wish Milly was here. She might have an idea."

Harry peered at the words. "It's a bit

like the message you get inside a fortune cookie — it could mean anything."

"It's useless." Jamie frowned. "How are we supposed to defeat the Gnome with a clue like that?" He shoved the book back into its drawer and slammed it shut.

Harry raised his eyebrows questioningly at Jamie.

"I'm all right," Jamie said, forcing a smile.

Harry sniffed the air. "Mmm," he said. "Can you smell something?"

"Boys! It's your favourite. Bacon and eggs!" Their mum's voice just reached them from the kitchen.

"Come on," said Harry. He pushed past Jamie towards the study door.

Jamie turned to race after him . . . but a high-pitched squeal stopped them both in their tracks. They froze and looked at each other. Jamie gulped. Was it the Gnome's rat? He looked carefully all around the room, listening hard, ready to bolt.

Nothing moved.

"Looks like those are the only rats here, Jamie," Harry said, pointing at one of the corners of the ceiling. A long line of rats was engraved into the plaster, scurrying over one another, their long tails flying. Harry frowned. "That wasn't there before," he said. "I'm sure it wasn't."

"Welcome to Gnome Gardens, Harry," Jamie told him. "Nothing makes any sense here. You should know that by now."

They went back into the secret passageway, closing the study door behind them.

*

Jamie swallowed his last mouthful of bacon. "Come on, let's get going."

Harry wiped some bread around his empty plate to mop up the last of his egg. He pushed it into his mouth, runny yolk dribbling down his chin. Jamie grabbed their empty plates and stacked them next to the sink.

"Bye, Mum! We're going to Milly's!" Jamie called. He heard his mum's muffled reply from the living room. On the way out Harry grabbed the backpack he always carried. *No doubt stuffed with all sorts of crazy objects,* Jamie thought.

He and Harry raced through the back door and out into the overgrown garden. The patchy grass came up to their waists in some places. They swished through it as they ran down the hill towards Gardener's

Cottage, the pretty, red-tiled house where Milly lived.

Harry got there first and rang the doorbell. A moment later Milly appeared, tucking a lock of her thick brown hair behind an ear. She smiled, but Jamie could see dark rings underneath her eyes.

"You all right, Milly?" he asked.

"Fine," she said brightly, coming out of the house and shutting the door behind her.

"Are you sure?" Jamie said.

Milly looked at him and Harry, then at the ground. "I can't sleep," she said. "It started when the bats came and got me from my bedroom. Now, whenever a pipe rattles, or a floorboard creaks, I think it's the Gnome coming to get me. Or more of his disgusting creatures."

"I'm not surprised," Jamie said. "Those bats were horrible. At least the scratches have almost gone – you can hardly see them now."

Milly touched her face, still showing very faint scratch marks from the bats' claws.

"What did you tell your mum and dad?" Harry asked, his eyes wide.

"That I had a nightmare and managed to scratch my face with my fingernails," Milly said, smiling thinly as she led the way down her garden path.

"And they believed you?" Jamie said.

"I know. It sounds a bit far-fetched, but it was the best I could do at the time," Milly said. "They've been watching me like hawks and asking me all sorts of questions ever since. But it's sort of true. I really am having nightmares — about the Gnome coming down the chimney in our living room and grabbing me." She shuddered.

Poor Milly, Jamie thought, as he closed the garden gate behind him. "We'll have to face him again soon," he said. "But we're tough enough. We'll be fine."

"Rats next," said Harry. "We thought we heard one squeal."

Jamie swallowed hard. "And we need to find the Gnome's rat if we're going to defeat him."

"Well, it's obvious where we should look first," said Milly, clambering over a rotting log.

Jamie and Harry glanced at each other. Milly rolled her eyes.

"In the ditch, of course!" she said. "That's

where rat runs usually are. Didn't you even know that? Come on!" She strode off into the overgrown garden.

Jamie and Harry smiled and shrugged at each other, then followed Milly through the grounds of Gnome Gardens. Jamie would never have said it to her face, but Milly could be a bit of a know-it-all sometimes.

The garden of the big house was on a steep slope, with terraces cut into the hill, and paths and steps snaking all over it. Tucked among the sprawling plants was a big abandoned greenhouse, and ancient sheds slowly falling apart. As they walked through the weeds and brambles at the bottom of the hill, Jamie looked up at the old grey-stone house above them, its windows like scowling eyes. A lightning-blasted tree stood in front of it, black branches thrusting into the sky.

"Phew! What's that?" asked Harry, wrinkling his nose.

"Stagnant water," said Milly. "Must be the ditch."

There was a sucking sound as the ground beneath their feet became muddier, pulling at their shoes.

"Careful you don't slide down the slope!" said Jamie.

Milly stopped beside a patch of nettles. "Here it is." She pushed back the nettles with a stick. "Down there."

Jamie could see a muddy brown trickle of water, almost hidden by the undergrowth. A cloud of gnats hung over it, buzzing.

"What does a 'rat run' look like, anyway?" Harry asked.

"Like a little path," Milly said. "The rats use the same routes over and over again when they go looking for food."

Something rustled in the weeds, very close. Jamie froze. He glanced at Milly and Harry. Slowly, the three of them crept towards the sound. More rustling. Jamie stared at the undergrowth, his heart pounding, waiting for a huge, filthy rat to leap out at him. There was another scrabbling sound and a startled quack; then a duck flapped clumsily into the air and away. Jamie let out a long breath.

He noticed a dull glint of metal in the undergrowth where the duck had been hiding and went to investigate. He kicked away some of the weeds to reveal a large iron disc set into the ground.

"What's that?" Harry asked over Jamie's shoulder.

Jamie gulped. "It's a manhole cover," he said, his voice hoarse. "I think it must lead to a sewer."

"Rats live in sewers," said Milly quietly.

They pushed aside more of the long grass and weeds. The manhole cover had some kind of decoration on it. Jamie brushed away the mud smeared over its surface. Then he stopped and staggered backwards.

From the middle of the iron cover sneered the ugly face of the Gnome.

CHAPTER THREE

Into the Sewer

Jamie, Harry and Milly stared down at the image of the Gnome's ugly face. There was a crack in the lid, from one side to the other, tracing the line of his twisted smile. It was big enough for Jamie to poke his finger inside – not that he wanted to. The manhole looked exactly like the sort of thing Mum was always warning them to stay away from.

"The Gnome's face. It always means trouble. He must be close," Milly said, frowning.

"Look!" said Harry. Something long and thin poked up from the crack in the cover. Was it a spider's leg?

But more quivering thin lines emerged, and in the centre of them was a tiny pink nose, sniffing the air. The rest of the creature squeezed itself out from the crack and ran towards them. A mouse, with sleek grey fur and long whiskers. It sat on its hind legs, looking up at them with shining brown eyes. Jamie felt relieved that it wasn't the big, ugly rat he'd been expecting. But he still didn't like it. Weren't mice usually terrified of people?

"Aw, it's so cute," said Harry. "Hello, little mouse." He leaned down and stretched his hand out to it.

Jamie grabbed the strap on Harry's backpack and pulled him back. "Don't, Harry!"

"It's only a mouse," Harry said, shaking Jamie's hand away.

The tiny creature darted off into the long grass.

"We have to be careful. What if the Gnome sent it?"

Harry looked at his brother. "You're not *scared* of a titchy little *mouse*, are you?" He laughed.

Jamie felt his cheeks grow hot. "It's not that—" he began.

A loud scraping sound made him turn towards Milly. She was trying to shift one of the iron halves of the manhole cover.

"Ooof," she gasped. "Heavier than it looks." She heaved at one of the pieces and managed to move it a few centimetres.

"Careful," Jamie said. "You'll hurt yourself." He didn't know how Milly could bear to touch the Gnome's ugly image. Who knew what was underneath it?

Milly wiped the sweat from her forehead with the back of her hand. "Do you two want to defeat the Gnome or not?"

Jamie and Harry knelt beside her and they all three tried to push the cover on to the grass. The piece Milly was pushing snapped loudly and cracked in two, clattering down into the opening. It sent out a huge splashing sound as it landed in the darkness below. She took a step back. The other piece cracked too and crashed noisily after it.

An uneasy feeling bubbled in Jamie's stomach. All three of them peered down into the murky hole. A sour smell wafted towards them and Harry held his nose. Water dripped noisily into the slimy brown sludge just visible at the bottom.

"It's a sewer all right," said Milly. She shuddered. "Urgh, imagine being trapped inside it."

"Who's going down first?" Harry asked.

Jamie burst out laughing. "You're joking," he said. "We've been down wells, up chimneys and trapped in attics. Every time, that evil Gnome has been there with his disgusting monsters, trying to kill us. And now you think it's a good idea to climb down into a stinking, rat-infested sewer? Mum warned us about manhole covers. They're not safe."

"Safe?" Harry spluttered. "We haven't been safe since we moved to Gnome Gardens!"

"But there's no point in looking for trouble, is there?" Jamie said.

Harry straightened his backpack. "But we'll *always* be in trouble unless we stand up to the Gnome and the rest of his creatures. We might as well do it now."

Milly shrugged. "At least it's not the middle of the night, like it usually is."

Jamie knew his little brother was right, but another look down into the gloom made him hesitate. He imagined being chased through the tunnels of the sewer, rats nipping at his heels. . .

Jamie felt a huge shove on his back.

His knees buckled and his legs gave way underneath him. He lunged forwards into empty air. *I'm falling in!* He felt his body tip over the edge, into the foul-smelling, dark opening.

"Ow!" he groaned as he landed painfully on his back, sludge and stagnant water seeping into his clothes. Jamie shuddered as he felt a furry body brush past him. He sat up, looking around in panic for the rat, just as Milly crashed down on top of him, followed by Harry. Jamie gasped, the wind knocked out of him. Milly had fallen badly, knocking the points of her elbows into his ribs, and Harry was in a heap beside him. The three of them lay in a tangle of arms and legs. Jamie heard another squeal. He felt sick.

"Someone pushed us," said Harry in a small voice.

The sludge made a horrible squelching sound as the three of them struggled to disentangle themselves and get to their feet. Jamie hurt all over. Slowly, they looked up at the disc of blue sky showing through the manhole.

The sky suddenly disappeared, blocked by a familiar, wicked face. The Gnome stared down into the sewer with dull red eyes. They could see his familiar red cap and his wispy, tangled beard.

"How nice of you to drop in," the Gnome cackled. His wrinkled face twisted into a satisfied sneer as he tapped a foot against the rim of the opening – the same foot that had kicked them all in.

Jamie felt Harry grip his elbow.

"Rats in a trap," spat the Gnome.

Jamie felt a wave of revulsion as he noticed a mouse scurrying over the Gnome's shoulder, whiskers twitching. The creature disappeared into the Gnome's shirt pocket with a flick of its grey tail. *It's the mouse from earlier*, Jamie realized.

"What's he going to do to us?" whimpered Harry. "He'll send the rats! He'll—"

"Quiet!" Milly whispered. Her face was white with fear. "Can you hear that?"

Jamie listened. A gurgling sound reached them along the pipe. Before Jamie could say anything, a sudden rush of filthy water came crashing into them.

"Help!" cried Harry.

Ferocious waves knocked them off their

feet. Jamie turned and twisted as his body slammed down, trying to swim against the push of water. But the surge was too powerful. As they were washed away down the sewer, Jamie could hear the Gnome's evil cackle echoing after them. "Goodbye, little fools!" he cried. "Have a nice swim!"

CHAPTER FOUR

The Raging River

"Ow!" Jamie cried out as he bashed painfully against the slimy side of the sewer. They were being swept along through the pipe so fast that the force of the water kept driving them into the walls.

"Try to stay in the middle!" shouted Milly from somewhere behind Jamie.

"Then you won't get knocked against the sides."

Jamie hurtled along, fighting to keep his face above the dirty, ice-cold water. As the pipe rounded a bend the water swirled, spinning him round. He caught sight of Harry, his hair plastered to his head, and Milly's pale white face.

"Jamie!" Harry cried, reaching out a hand. Jamie tried to grab it, but the churning waters swept him further away from his brother. The water sent out a stink of rotten eggs and other things that Jamie didn't want to think about.

The sewer was lit with an eerie green light that seemed to be coming from the slime on the walls, and reflected on the water's filthy surface. Jamie noticed, with a shudder, that the topmost bricks were carved with rats, running in a continuous line along the sewer.

The pipe made another sharp turn, catching Jamie's shoulder painfully. For a moment a column of daylight sliced down into the murk, and he realized they were at the bottom of the old well, where they'd met the Gnome's terrifying snakes. He reached out for the bucket that dangled on a chain down the shaft, but the water swept him onwards.

This sewer wasn't here last time we were in the well, he remembered. He thought of the complex network of tunnels inside the walls of Gnome Gardens, where they had been chased by the Gnome's spider. *It's as if the Gnome is joining up all the tunnels.*

He spluttered through the spray, wondering what evil plan their enemy was hatching.

A squeak made Jamie look to his left. To his horror, a rat as big as his head was being swept along, so close he could have touched it. The rat squealed and scrambled on to a ledge.

"Watch out!" cried Jamie over the sound of the rushing water, as they hurtled round another bend. Light filled the pipe. It was the end of the sewer!

Jamie shot out of the tunnel in an arc of filthy spray and foam. He landed with a huge splash in an expanse of churning brown water. He blinked, his eyes adjusting to the bright daylight, as Harry and Milly tumbled after him. Harry pulled a face as he spat out a mouthful of water. His backpack hung heavily on his shoulders, waterlogged. He and Milly bobbed beside Jamie, their faces pale and frightened.

"We're in the River Bluff," Milly gasped. "Be careful, there can be dangerous currents."

The surface was calm, but beneath it Jamie could feel the pull of the river, dragging him under. It felt like an octopus was holding him in its tentacles. "We've got to get to the bank," he said.

They swam through the dark green water. Although Jamie kicked hard and moved his arms as powerfully as he could, he felt as if he was hardly moving. Great, fat raindrops plopped into the river. They drummed into Jamie's head like tiny, icy hammers, making him feel even colder. His teeth began to chatter. His sodden clothes felt heavier and heavier. He looked at Milly and Harry. Their faces were tinged with blue and they could barely lift their arms out of the water. *We have to get out, and get dry*, Jamie thought, *or we'll die of cold.*

The bank was steep and slick with brown mud. Trees grew along it, their branches hanging down over the water, but they were way out of reach. How were they going to get out of the river? *This is all my fault*, Jamie thought. *If I hadn't been peering down into the sewer, imagining rats, the Gnome wouldn't have been able to kick us in.*

"Help!" Harry cried.

Jamie turned to see Harry struggling desperately. His brother had the added weight of the heavy backpack, which

Jamie could see was beginning to drag him underwater.

"Don't worry, Harry." Jamie stopped treading water for a moment, and let the current carry him back towards his brother.

"Here!" Milly grabbed his arm as he passed her. They both drifted back to Harry, who was swimming furiously against the current when they reached him. *Good old Harry.* He never gave up, even when their adventures turned really nasty.

"Got you," Jamie panted as he grabbed his brother's shoulder and struggled to pull off one of the backpack's straps. Harry slipped under the surface of the water. Jamie hoisted him up again and he gasped for breath.

"I'll hold him up, you get the backpack off," Milly told Jamie through chattering teeth. She grasped Harry around the waist.

"Anything useful in it?" Jamie asked as he slipped the second strap off Harry's arm.

Harry shook his head. But before Jamie could let it go, he yelled, "Wait!"

Jamie gripped the straps firmly to keep the current from sweeping it away.

"Skipping rope," gasped Harry.

"Harry, you're a genius," Jamie said, grinning. "That's just what we need! We can use it to grab on to one of those trees." He felt around in the bag for the wooden-handled rope, pulled it out and let the current drag the backpack away.

"Quick!" Milly said. "Over that branch."

Jamie held one handle and flung the other towards the shore, kicking against the swirling current. The rope flopped uselessly into the water. He tried again. This time, the wooden handle caught in the fork between two large branches. Jamie gave it a tug and it stayed.

"You did it!" cried Harry. When Jamie looked round he could see his brother's chest heaving with the effort of staying afloat.

"One at a time – I don't think it's strong enough for all of us," Jamie said. "You go first, Harry. Grab the rope and get yourself to the bank while I hold it taut."

Harry caught hold of the skipping rope and used it to pull himself to the riverbank, hand over hand. When he got to the shore he checked that the handle of the rope was still firmly stuck in the tree, then waved at Jamie and Milly. His head bobbed up and down in the water as he clung to a root sticking out of the bank.

"You go next," said Milly, gasping.

Jamie shook his head firmly. "No time to argue," he said. He heaved the rope tight again and watched as Milly pulled herself along it to the shore, feeling the muscles in his arms begin to give way. To his relief, Milly and Harry both took the other end of the rope and began to pull. He felt his body moving through the water, his legs trailing behind him. They were pulling him in! He was so exhausted when he got to them he flopped against the soft mud of the bank. He could feel his whole body trembling. If he felt this bad, how did the others feel?

"You two OK?" he asked. Milly nodded, her mouth set in a determined line. Harry hesitated, then sent him a shaky smile and a thumbs up.

"The water's still deep here, but there's not much current," Harry said through chattering teeth. "I've been looking for somewhere to climb out but it's all too slippery."

They tried to pull themselves on to the muddy shore. Their hands slid about, trying to find a grip, but mud squelched up between their fingers and Jamie's toes kept losing grip so that his body slammed into the oozing mud over and over. Milly grasped a tussock of grass but the weight of her body tore it up by its roots. They were slipping back into the water.

"What are we going to do?" Harry whimpered.

"There must be a way out – keep looking,"

Jamie said, putting a hand to his brother's arm. "Maybe further up this way."

They pulled themselves along the steep bank as best they could. "Look!" shouted Milly. "There's a tunnel."

Sure enough, there was a large hole cut into the muddy bank, like the burrow of a huge rabbit. They peered inside. Instead of pointing down into the earth, the tunnel was angled upwards, towards the top of the bank.

"I'm not going in any more tunnels," said Harry.

Jamie looked at his brother. It was easy to see why Harry wasn't feeling so brave now: he was shivering, soaked, and there were streaks of mud all over his face.

"It's the only way out of here," said Milly.

"I'll go first."

She heaved herself up and into the hole. First her body and then her legs disappeared from view. Jamie stared after her, holding his breath. A few moments later, they heard her voice above their heads.

"Come on! It's easy!" Milly was standing at the top of the bank, covered in mud, waving down at them. Her hair was plastered to the sides of her face.

Jamie let out a long breath. "Go on, Harry. You go next."

Harry pulled himself into the tunnel and scrambled upwards. Jamie waited until Harry emerged safely alongside Milly, then heaved himself into the narrow opening.

He had just managed to get his head and shoulders inside the tunnel when he felt a great glob of mud land on the back of his neck. Then another. There was a splattering sound as more mud began to fall. The tunnel was collapsing! *I've got to get out of here*, he realized, his heart thumping. Quickly Jamie wriggled backwards, tipping back into the cold, churning river. The end of the tunnel collapsed in, forming a slick of oozing mud that slid down into the river. Jamie could see Harry and Milly looking down at him from the top of the bank. His only chance of joining them had disappeared. With a *plop!* a last globule of mud landed in the water before him. Needles of rain drove into his cheeks, harder than ever.

"What's happened?" called Harry. He and Milly were stamping their feet and hugging themselves to warm up. Their worried faces seemed very far away.

"The tunnel's caved in," Jamie shouted. What could he do now? The only way out of the icy river had just disappeared. He began shivering more violently than before.

He looked around frantically as his feet trod water. There had to be another way out! A long, thick cord slipped down the muddy bank towards him. A rope! Where had Harry and Milly found it? Jamie reached out to grab it – then some instinct made him snatch his hand back. He shuddered, unable to move. It wasn't a rope. It was pinkish-grey with a few bristly hairs sticking out from it. It seemed familiar. Like a long, fat tail.

The tail of a giant rat.

CHAPTER FIVE

The Giant Rat

Jamie shrank back, his stomach churning. He looked up at Milly and Harry.

They had both twisted round and were staring over their shoulders at something. Milly had put a comforting arm around Harry, drawing him to her. The rat. Jamie could see it now. They were up there with a giant rat! Its whiskers quivered in the rain and its thick, greasy coat clung to its ribs as its claws dug into the mud. The rat's bulbous pink eyes were watching Jamie.

Milly looked over at him. Her eyes were wide with fear. "You've no choice, Jamie," she called. "You'll have to climb the tail."

Jamie was so wet, so cold and so tired that he almost didn't have the energy left to feel disgusted. *Almost*. He swallowed hard and put out a hand to the thick, ribbed tail. It was cold to the touch and slimy from the mud. The sparse hairs felt coarse. Jamie gripped on to it and began to climb, dragging himself up one hand over the other, his feet scrabbling against the muddy bank. He felt even colder out of the water. But Jamie knew he must keep going.

The tail twitched underneath his hands and he almost let go, revolted.

"You can do it!" called Harry from the top of the bank.

"You're almost there!" cried Milly.

Jamie almost wanted to yell out and warn them both to stay safe from the huge rat, but the animal was as still as a statue, watching. *Strange*, thought Jamie. *Why isn't he attacking?* That's what all the other Gnome creatures had done.

He tightened his grip on the slimy pink tail. Exhausted, he reached the top of the bank and collapsed on to the grass, lying on his front. Harry and Milly sat next to him, rubbing his back to help warm him.

"You're all right now," said Milly. "We'll get out of this."

For a moment, all Jamie could do was stare at the blades of grass in front of his nose. He'd made it. The rain had stopped, and he felt sunshine warm his shoulders. Wearily, he climbed to his hands and knees, helped by Harry and Milly.

Now he could see the rat up close. It was a huge brown creature, crouched in the weeds, its tail still dangling down the riverbank. Jamie only just managed not to scream. The rat was twice as big as the three of them put together. Bigger than the monster spider, and even bigger than the giant snake. On the rat's head was a golden crown, just like in the picture from *The Book of Gnome*, and round its neck was a collar embedded with coloured jewels. The Rat King opened its jaws to lick long teeth that looked as though they could slice Jamie in two. Its eyes glittered and its haunches tensed, as if it was about to make a great leap.

"It hasn't hurt us," Harry said.

"Yet," added Milly.

Jamie gulped, fighting down a wave of nausea. He realized he was still on one knee, gripping Milly's and Harry's arms tightly. He forced himself to look around, to get an idea of where they were. He could just glimpse Gnome Gardens in the distance, over the matted fur on the rat's shoulder. Mum and Dad would never hear them if they called for help from here.

"Come on, let's get behind that tree," Milly said.

Jamie climbed shakily to his feet and ran to join the other two behind a big oak. They peered round it. The rat was watching, its nose quivering as it sniffed the air. It took a few scuttling steps towards them, its huge claws kicking up clods of turf.

"It could easily get us. It's enormous; it must be ten times faster than we are," said Harry. "Why isn't it attacking?"

"And why did it help me climb out of the river?" wondered Jamie.

"Maybe it's waiting for the Gnome," suggested Milly.

The rat opened its mouth, revealing long yellow teeth, bits of rancid food embedded between them. The horrible stench of its breath, like rotting meat, wafted towards them. It let out a loud, shrieking squeal. Huge fleas leaped over its fur.

"Yuck," said Harry in a muffled voice. His

hand was over his mouth. Jamie covered his nose. The rat was staring straight at him, its bulbous eyes shining.

"Look," said Milly. "Its collar. There's a chain attached. Maybe—"

Before Milly could finish her sentence, a vicious tug on the chain made the rat lurch backwards, knocked off its feet. It struggled to right itself, its long claws raking the air, and gave a cry that Jamie thought was half angry, half anguished. The chain was golden, like the crown, and snaked from the rat's collar back into the undergrowth. There was another tug. The rat got to its feet and was dragged towards the bushes as the links of the chain were pulled in.

"I think I know who's at the other end of

the chain," Milly said. Her eyes were wide. "The Gnome."

"There's only one way to find out for sure," said Harry.

"Come on, then," Jamie said, stepping out from behind the tree. He had to be brave, even if he was scared of rats. "Let's follow."

CHAPTER SIX

The Abandoned Graveyard

The rat disappeared into woodland thick with brambles. They had to run to keep up with it. *Of all the things I could be chasing after*, Jamie thought, *I can't believe it's a gigantic, filthy rat!* At least the running was warming him up. His clothes stuck to him, still sodden with river water, but the sun was helping to dry him off.

"I know these woods," Milly said, panting along behind Jamie. "We're near Far Monkton." That was the neighbouring village to theirs.

They glimpsed the rat as it scurried out of the undergrowth, on to a narrow path, and crashed into another patch of bushes. The squawk of a crow made Jamie look up: a black church spire was silhouetted above him, through the trees, its weathervane broken and bent.

"That's Saint Saviour's church," Milly said.

The trees thinned and they followed the rustling bushes to the churchyard entrance. They stopped, panting for breath. There was no sign of the rat.

"It must have gone in there," said Milly, pointing at the open gate.

They stepped inside. Ancient gravestones leaned towards one another in wonky rows, the words carved into them worn smooth with time. Twisting paths led among the graves, overgrown with brambles and nettles. Unseen creatures rustled in the undergrowth, but the rat seemed to have vanished.

They stood by an ivy-covered gravestone. The old church loomed above them, completely derelict. It leaned at a dangerous angle, shattered stained glass and rotten wood lying on the ground around it, its windows and doors boarded up.

"It hasn't been used for years," Milly said.

In front of them Jamie noticed a fallen

gargoyle smashed on the ground.

"Look," said Harry. "Narrow eyes, wispy beard, the nose with warts on. And look at the cap. It looks like. . ."

"The Gnome," Milly finished for him.

Mocking laughter echoed around the gravestones. At the same moment the sun slipped behind a dark cloud.

Jamie spun around, searching for the Gnome. But all he could see were the overgrown graves.

"There," whispered Harry, pointing with a shaking finger.

In a corner of the churchyard, at the end of a narrow path, stood an elaborate stone tomb decorated with angels. On the flat top of the tomb perched a small, thin figure holding a chain. The Gnome. His legs hung over the side, his long yellow toenails scratching against the grey stone. He was wearing his usual yellow shirt and green trousers and there were flecks of spittle in his wispy beard. The Gnome was staring at them, his eyes narrowed. He pulled on the chain and the giant rat lurched into view from behind the tomb.

"I believe you've met my royal friend," he snarled. He yanked savagely at the chain, making the rat's head knock against the stone. "I can see you like rats. Especially *you*." He pointed a bony finger at Jamie.

The King Rat met Jamie's gaze and held it for a moment, then shifted its glittering eyes to look above them. The rat glanced back down without moving its head, almost as if it wanted to check that Jamie was watching.

It's almost as if the rat is trying to tell me something, Jamie thought. *But why would it want to help me?*

"Perhaps you'd like to meet some of King Rat's friends," the Gnome continued, jangling the chain. Jamie could see six or seven ordinary-sized rats scurrying across the tomb. One ran over the Gnome's legs. It was all Jamie could do not to cry out. *Stay brave*, he told himself. *You can do this.* He had to defeat the Gnome – he didn't want Milly to keep having nightmares or for Harry to always worry about what was round the corner. There was only one way to stop them all from being frightened, and that was to get rid of the Gnome once and for all. If he could just keep going. . .

Suddenly, the Gnome reached into his

pocket and pulled out a coarse-looking, thick rope. It slipped through the Gnome's hands as if it were oiled. Jamie frowned, and felt another wave of sickness. Surely it couldn't be. . .

"It looks like it's made from greasy hair," said Milly. "It's disgusting."

The Gnome whirled the rope in a circle above his head.

"What's he doing?" said Harry.

"Run!" yelled Jamie.

But as they turned to flee, the Gnome's horrible lasso whipped through the air and with a *whoosh!* encircled the three of them in its greasy loop. He yanked it tight around their ankles and jerked, pulling them to the ground.

The Gnome hauled on the rope, bumping

them across the rough path on their backs. How could such a little man be so strong? Jamie tried to sit up but the Gnome was pulling them along too fast. Brambles clawed at his clothes and skin. He squirmed and kicked his legs, trying uselessly to loosen the thick hair rope that bound their ankles.

"Jamie!" Harry cried. "Stop him!" But there was nothing Jamie could do.

"You stupid little wretches," snarled the Gnome as he pulled them towards him. "When" – he grunted with effort – "are you going to" – he grunted again – "*learn*?"

The Gnome stopped pulling when they were close to the tomb. Jamie sat up and saw that there was a pit beside them. It was deep – more than twice his height. High bushes grew around it, dense with vicious-looking spines. He looked at Molly. A trickle of blood ran from her lip, but when she saw him notice she frowned.

"I'm fine," she whispered. "Don't worry about me."

The sound of squeaking echoed up from the pit. Jamie felt colder than ever. *Rats*, he thought. *It must be*. He shuddered and leaned to look at the bottom of the pit. It was a writhing mass of rats. They climbed over each other, wriggling and squirming, long tails snaking through the air and whiskers quivering. It made Jamie's skin itch just to look at them.

"He's going to shove us in there with them!" whimpered Harry.

"No one will find you," said the Gnome.

"Not here, in this deserted graveyard. There's no one to hear you. Soon you'll be no more trouble to me." He yanked on the giant rat's chain again. "Be sure to make yourself comfortable, because you'll be staying a very long time . . . while I go and live in Gnome Gardens!" His voice had risen to a shout, his wrinkled face flushed with triumph.

"Mum and Dad won't let you live there!" Harry called desperately.

The Gnome flashed them an evil grin, revealing yellow-stained and broken teeth. "They won't have a choice," he said.

Jamie gulped and peered into the pit. His stomach churned. The pit walls were steep and slippery with mud and slime, with a mouldy root sticking out here and there, grey and dead. A horrible, stagnant smell wafted up from the bottom, where hundreds of black and brown rats crawled over one another, squealing shrilly, their fur matted with mud and filth. Some of them clambered up the steep sides of the pit only to topple back in, but most scrambled about in the bottom, a dense mass of furry bodies.

"What a nightmare," Jamie whispered. Almost straightaway, he wished he could snatch the words back. He glanced up at Milly and Harry's faces, and saw that they'd heard. Harry looked close to tears and a frown creased Milly's brow. Jamie tried to swallow but his throat had turned dry.

"What do we do now?" Harry asked.

Jamie shook his head. He could feel his whole body trembling. "I don't know."

CHAPTER SEVEN

The Rat Pit

Jamie could hear the Gnome grunting behind him and turned round. He was fixing the end of the greasy rope around a stone angel on the tomb, tying it in a complicated knot. How were they going to get away?

"We're trapped," Harry whimpered. "We're

going to end up in that horrible rat pit. Look at their teeth."

The Gnome was still holding the King Rat's chain. Jamie's eyes followed it to the rat's jewelled collar. The creature's glassy red eyes stared at him, then flicked upwards again. The rat was signalling to Jamie, he was sure of it.

"The King Rat's looking at something," Milly whispered.

But what could it be? The sky? It was empty. The church, towering above them? It looked as creepy as the pit.

There was a pause. The rat flicked its eyes again, and sunlight glinted on its golden crown.

"That's it!" Harry whispered excitedly.

Of course! The Gnome loved shiny

things – even knives and forks were like treasure to him.

"It must be the most precious thing the Gnome owns," Milly said. She glanced down at the pit, one eyebrow raised. "I bet he'd hate to lose it down there."

"He'd jump in after it," said Harry.

Jamie nodded. It would have to work – it was the only plan they had. "You two get this rope untied," he whispered. "I'll distract the Gnome."

Milly and Harry began pulling at the greasy rope that was digging into their ankles.

"Struggle all you like," sneered the Gnome, jumping down from the tomb. "You won't get away."

"Hey!" Jamie called to him. From the

corner of his eye, he could see Milly reaching out as far as she could towards a broken branch, vicious spines sticking out of it like thick black needles. He couldn't let the Gnome see her. "Your pet doesn't look very happy," he said.

The Gnome turned to the giant rat, which cowered, dipping its head. He gave a savage yank on the golden chain. The rat squealed, showing its long teeth.

Jamie could just see Milly reach the prickly branch. Harry held the hair rope still while she hacked at it with the spines. Jamie waved his arms, keeping the Gnome focused on him.

"You don't scare us," he said. "That mangy creature couldn't hurt a fly."

The Gnome pointed a bony finger at

Jamie, its yellow nail curled grotesquely. "We'll see how you feel when you're in the pit," he spat, his scowling face red with rage. "There are hundreds of my rats down there, and they're feeling hungry."

Jamie felt the rope suddenly slacken.

"Done it!" said Milly triumphantly, kicking the rope away from their ankles. "Come on!"

Jamie jumped to his feet, pulling Harry with him, and the three of them ran away from the pit towards the church. The Gnome let out a blood-chilling scream of fury.

"Now it's our turn to distract him," Milly panted to Jamie as they ran. "You get the crown."

She and Harry peeled off to one side, through the gravestones, weaving this way and that. The Gnome was after them like a terrier, spittle gathering at the corners of his mouth.

Jamie ran towards the giant rat. He swallowed hard as he approached the huge creature and the smell of it hit him. His stomach churned at the thought of climbing up that matted, stinking fur on to the rat's back – but he knew he had to do it.

"Hurry!" Jamie heard Harry shout. He glanced back and saw that the Gnome was gaining on them. He turned back to the rat. Its long claws were black with grime. He would have to stand on one of its feet and start climbing. He shuddered. But to his surprise the rat squatted down on its haunches and nodded its head at Jamie. *It's on our side!* Jamie thought. He remembered the words in *The Book of Gnome: The worst enemy can make a hidden friend.*

"I can trust you, can't I?" he said to the rat. It nodded once, as though in understanding. "What am I waiting for?" Jamie cried.

He grabbed a fistful of fur, fleas leaping at his touch. The rat didn't move as Jamie pulled himself up its great flank, then struggled up on to the creature's back, feeling the bones of its knobbly spine under his hands. He tried breathing through his mouth to avoid the terrible stench. *Poor thing,* he thought, *it's filthy and skinny.* Fleas jumped on to his damp sweatshirt and he brushed them away.

"It must be horrible being the Gnome's prisoner," Jamie muttered to the rat. "No wonder you want to get rid of him."

He reached out to the crown. It was a

perfect circle of gold, with five pointed tips. His fingertips brushed against it and he pushed. But the crown was hooked over one of the rat's ears and didn't budge. The King Rat tilted its head backwards, making the crown fall towards Jamie.

"Thanks!" Jamie buried his hands deep in the rat's filthy fur under the edge of the crown. He heaved it up.

"Gnome!" Jamie called. "I have your treasure!"

The Gnome turned towards Jamie. Then he froze, his mouth open in a terrible cry of rage.

CHAPTER EIGHT

Rat Race

Jamie lifted the crown high above his head, then hurled it down into the pit.

"My treasure!" The Gnome screamed and ran towards it, leaving Milly and Harry panting behind him among the gravestones.

Jamie jumped off the King Rat's back in a wide arc and landed next to the pit.

"What have you done?" cried the Gnome. He leaped down into the pit, rats squealing as he landed on them, and looked around desperately for the crown.

"You all right?" asked Milly, as she and Harry joined Jamie.

Jamie nodded. He felt Milly brushing a hand down his back. He shuddered. It must be covered with those huge rat fleas.

"We saw you get on the rat's back," Harry said. "You were brilliant." His voice was full of admiration.

"It's not over yet," Jamie muttered.

There was a clunking sound. The King Rat's jewelled collar had fallen to the ground. The giant creature gave a high-pitched cry that sounded almost like a shout of triumph.

"It's free!" Jamie cried. "Now the Gnome's trapped in the pit, maybe he's lost his power over the rat."

The rat turned to Jamie, Harry and Milly. It shook itself, and Jamie could see the cruel marks on its neck where the chain had worn away the fur. Slowly, the rat nodded at them, its eyes looking into theirs, before scuttling off between the gravestones into the tall undergrowth.

"Got it!" The Gnome's voice echoed up from the pit. Jamie looked over the side to see the Gnome standing waist-deep in rats, cradling the crown. Rats scurried over his scrawny body. The crown and the Gnome's arms were caked in thick mud.

"Out of my way!" shrieked the Gnome, kicking rats right and left as he made for the side of the pit. The mud walls towered above him.

"He'll never get out of there," Milly said. "It's too deep."

She was right. The sides of the pit were sheer and slick with wet mud. The Gnome waded through the rats to a muddy wall and tried to find a grip. He gave a cry of rage as he slithered back down among the rats.

"Curse you!" he shouted, waving a gnarled fist. He put the crown down, and began pulling handfuls of wet mud away from the walls, packing them together to make a step. "You haven't seen the last of me!" he shouted.

"Come on," said Jamie. "Let's go before he escapes."

"My rats will get you!" screamed the

Gnome. "Creatures, after them!"

Jamie, Harry and Millie looked at one another, then at the pit. Jamie felt his stomach lurch as twenty or so rats leaped out over the side and on to the path. They began scurrying towards the children, squealing, their yellow teeth snapping. More followed, until a seething carpet of rats was racing towards them.

"Run!" Jamie shouted.

They pelted through the graveyard. Jamie felt his heart thumping as he sprinted between the gravestones, leaping over brambles and swerving lumps of broken glass and wood.

Harry stumbled on a tree root and as Jamie grabbed his arm he risked a glance behind him. Hundreds of rats were after them, a horrible tide of filthy fur leaping along only a few strides away, squealing shrilly as they came. "Quick!" he shouted, pulling Harry along, out of the graveyard and into a narrow lane.

"They've stopped!" shouted Milly, slowing her pace.

Jamie looked behind him. The rats were loping along slowly. Some were turning back. "We must be too far away from the Gnome for them to follow," he said.

"Keep running, though!" Harry panted. "Just in case."

They ran until they reached a crossroads with a signpost to their village. Everything was quiet and the sun glinted down between the branches of the trees. No one would ever believe what a horrid adventure they'd just had.

"Not far now," said Milly, leading the way along the road. For a few moments, they walked along in silence. Jamie's clothes were slowly drying in the sun, becoming stiff with all the dirt.

"I didn't know you hated rats so much, Jamie," Harry said after a while.

Jamie shuddered. "At least there's one good thing to come out of this," he said. "Well, two."

"What?" Harry asked.

"First, we defeated the rat – well, set it free, really."

Harry looked around him. "I wonder where the King Rat is now," he murmured.

"Second?" said Milly. Her lip had stopped bleeding now.

"Wherever the rat is, he's on our side.

Maybe the next creature will want to help us too," Jamie said.

"The Gnome's evil," Milly said, nodding, "so he's probably horrible to his creatures. Maybe they all hate him."

"I've lost my backpack because of him," said Harry glumly. "It'll be at the bottom of the river by now."

Milly slowed down and put an arm round him.

"Don't worry," said Jamie. "We'll get you a new one. You can find some more useful stuff to go in it."

Jamie could see the village green just along the road. They'd soon be home. "Let's find out what the next creature is when we get back," he said. "There's only one page left to turn in *The Book of*

Gnome. We've got this far; we can't give up now."

"The last battle," Harry said.

"When we defeat him for ever!" said Milly.

They passed the pond on the village green. A grey heron stood motionless on the bank, ready with its sharp long beak. The pond water glimmered dull green, gnats buzzing above its dark surface.

"*Croak!*"

Jamie looked down. A fat, warty toad had hopped on to the path. It stared up at them with bulging eyes.

"The King Rat looked at us like that," Jamie said, staring back. "It's as if it knows something."

The toad croaked again, then hopped

into the grass and away.

"Is that the next creepy creature?" Harry asked.

"Well," said Jamie, "there's only one way to find out. . ."